I JUST FORGOT

BY
MERCER MAYER

A Random House PICTUREBACK® Book

Random House 🏠 New York

I Just Forgot book, characters, text, and images © 1988 Mercer Mayer. LITTLE CRITTER, MERCER MAYER'S LITTLE CRITTER, and MERCER MAYER'S LITTLE CRITTER and Logo are registered trademarks of Orchard House Licensing Company. All rights reserved. Published in the United States by Random House Children's Books, a division of Random House, Inc., New York. Originally published in 1988 by Golden Books Publishing Company, Inc. PICTUREBACK, RANDOM HOUSE, and the Random House colophon are registered trademarks of Random House, Inc.
www.randomhouse.com/kids
Educators and librarians, for a variety of teaching tools, visit us at
www.randomhouse.com/teachers
Library of Congress Control Number: 87-81779
ISBN-10: 0-307-11975-0   ISBN-13: 978-0-307-11975-9
Printed in the United States of America
22 21 20 19
First Random House Edition 2006

For Benjamin

Sometimes I remember, and sometimes I just forget.

This morning I remembered to brush my teeth,
but I forgot to make my bed.

I put my dishes in the sink after breakfast, but I forgot to put the milk away.

I almost forgot to feed the puppy, but he reminded me.

Grrrr

I didn't forget to water the plants. They looked fine to me.

I didn't forget to feed the goldfish.
He just didn't look hungry. I'll
do it now, Mom.

I got ready for school.
I even got to the school bus on time.

But I forgot my lunch box.

Mom brought it to school for me.
Thanks, Mom.

After school, I went outside to play in the rain.
I remembered to put on my rain slicker.

But I forgot my rubber boots.

When I came inside for a snack, I didn't forget to take my boots off. I left them on because I was going right back outside.

I had cookies and milk.

I was just going to eat three cookies, but
I forgot to count them.

I didn't forget to shut the refrigerator door, though.
I just wasn't finished eating yet.

When Dad came home from work, I was supposed to get his paper. I didn't forget—the puppy got it first.

I know it's time for bed. I didn't forget.

Of course I'll remember to pick up my toys when
I'm finished playing with them.

I took my bath and remembered to wash behind my ears.

I didn't use soap, but I didn't forget to. I just don't like soap.

I guess I did forget to pick up my toys.

Did I forget to turn off the tub, too?

But there is one thing I never forget.

I always remember to have Mom
read me a bedtime story. And I always remember
to kiss her good night.